I0841049

TRENT MOTU

Master Of The Universe

Written By Author S.B. Three & Illustrated By Saira Riaz

Hunger Life Motu Publishing LLC Jackson, Michigan

To all you creative courageous children. Remember that all the miracles of the universe can be discovered within your mind! –S.B. Three

Copyright © 2023 by Hunger Life Motu Publishing LLC

Visit author S.B. Three website at www.hungerlifemotu.com

All rights reserved.

No part of this publication may be reproduced, distributed, or transmitted in any form or by any means, including photocopying, recording, or other electronic or mechanical methods, without the prior written permission of the publisher, except as permitted by U.S. copyright law. For permission requests, contact S.B.Three@hungerlifemotu.com

The Hunger Life Motu logo is a trademark of Hunger Life Motu Publishing LLC.

The story, all names, characters, and incidents portrayed in this production are fictitious. No identification with actual persons (living or deceased), places, buildings, and products is intended or should be inferred.

Book Cover by Saira Riaz

ISBN: 979-8-9887686-0-9   (Paperback)

ISBN: 979-8-9887686-1-6   (Ebook - EPUB)

Library of Congress Control Number: 2023913531

First Edition 2023

Chapter One

GOLD INSIDE MY BLOOD

Before he evolved and came to be known as Trent MOTU, his name was actually Tallrog. He was an 18ft tall young boy that came from a far Planet in the galaxy called Ta'tubulas. Planet Ta'tubulas is known to inhabit some of the most giant and powerful beings in the universe, but their life is very short on this

planet and this Tallrog knows. The planet grows stronger by absorbing half of all life forms on it in a random selection every 72 days. This is to renew itself and become greater.

Though the sacrifice for the planet is great & honorable, Tallrog wants to live a longer life and become more and also wished that his people had that same opportunity. He realized one day that he could be all that he believed he was destined for if he were to travel to a Planet called Earth. He found this out from visiting a temple nearby where 3 ancient wise Ta'tubulans resided. Their names were Vas, Ethra, & Didimus. These 3 ancient ones, had somehow been fortunate enough to have never been selected to be a part of the natural absorption on the planet yet, after many many cycles.

Tallrog believed that they could be the ones to help him so he went to the temple where they were. Tallrog told them of his concerns about

eventually being absorbed by the planet and that he has this desire to become more. They understood his troubles and they told him about a miraculous planet called Earth. "On planet Earth it has been reported that you can possibly live a very long life.

In fact, it has been said to believe that once a person enters that realm, they are likely to live forever," said Vas. Tallrog's face lit up with excitement. "This journey will not be an easy one though I must warn you," said Vas.

Tallrog eagerly asks the ancient ones, "please share more with me. What is it I must know to get there?" "Alright" they said, and with much knowledge they told him of another great planet nearby called Serutu that holds a special gear suit called Blasto Armor in a city called Ampullar.

The Ancient one Ethra said to him, "we can give you the coordinates, but you must know that intruders never make it past 5 days on planet Serutu.

This is because it is hard for anyone who isn't a natural inhabitant of that planet to breathe in its air any more than those 5 days. If you manage to get the Blasto Armor within 5 days it can extend time up to a year on Serutu but nothing further than that, no matter what.

The suit is intended for Earth. This is why there hasn't been any successful attempts yet."

They Told Tallrog that the suit would be his only chance towards surviving the risky entry upon planet Earth's atmosphere safely. If he makes it there safely with the suit, his body will then be able to naturally adapt to Earth's atmosphere once it comes off. "The other troublesome thing is that the city of Ampullar which holds the suit is also heavily guarded by soldiers," said the ancient one Didimus.

He then told Tallrog that he was already born with a protective suit called Zyo Armor that should allow him to travel to Serutu and be strong enough to help fight against any enemies trying to stop him on his quest towards the city Ampullar.

He told him that in order to activate it, he must place his whole body under this special water only found in their temple called Neme Water. "We can lead you to this water under one condition," said the Ancient one Vas. Tallrog eyes widened as he looked and said to him, "and what condition do you speak of." The ancient one Ethra replied.

"We only ask that if you see this journey through, you will share this story with the world about where you come from and how you decided to become the change that you wanted to see." The Ancient one Didimus then said. "Are you sure that this is the destiny that you seek?"

Tallrog thanked the elders for their concern and the knowledge they had just provided him with. He then said to them, "I am peace, I am love, I have Gold inside my blood. I am healthy, I am strong, I am worthy to belong. I am destined, I am brave, I believe I will see more days."

It is very clear that Tallrog was willing to take on the conditions in order to fulfill his life purpose of becoming more. He slowly but firmly replied "Yes-I-Am & Yes-I-Will". They then took him to the part of the temple where the Neme Water was located. He then rested his whole body inside of the Neme Water.

"Inhale deeply through your nose and exhale from your mouth six times, before holding on the seventh inhaled breath for 30 seconds. This will only work if you follow these instructions," said Vas. Tallrog closed his eyes and did as he was instructed to do.

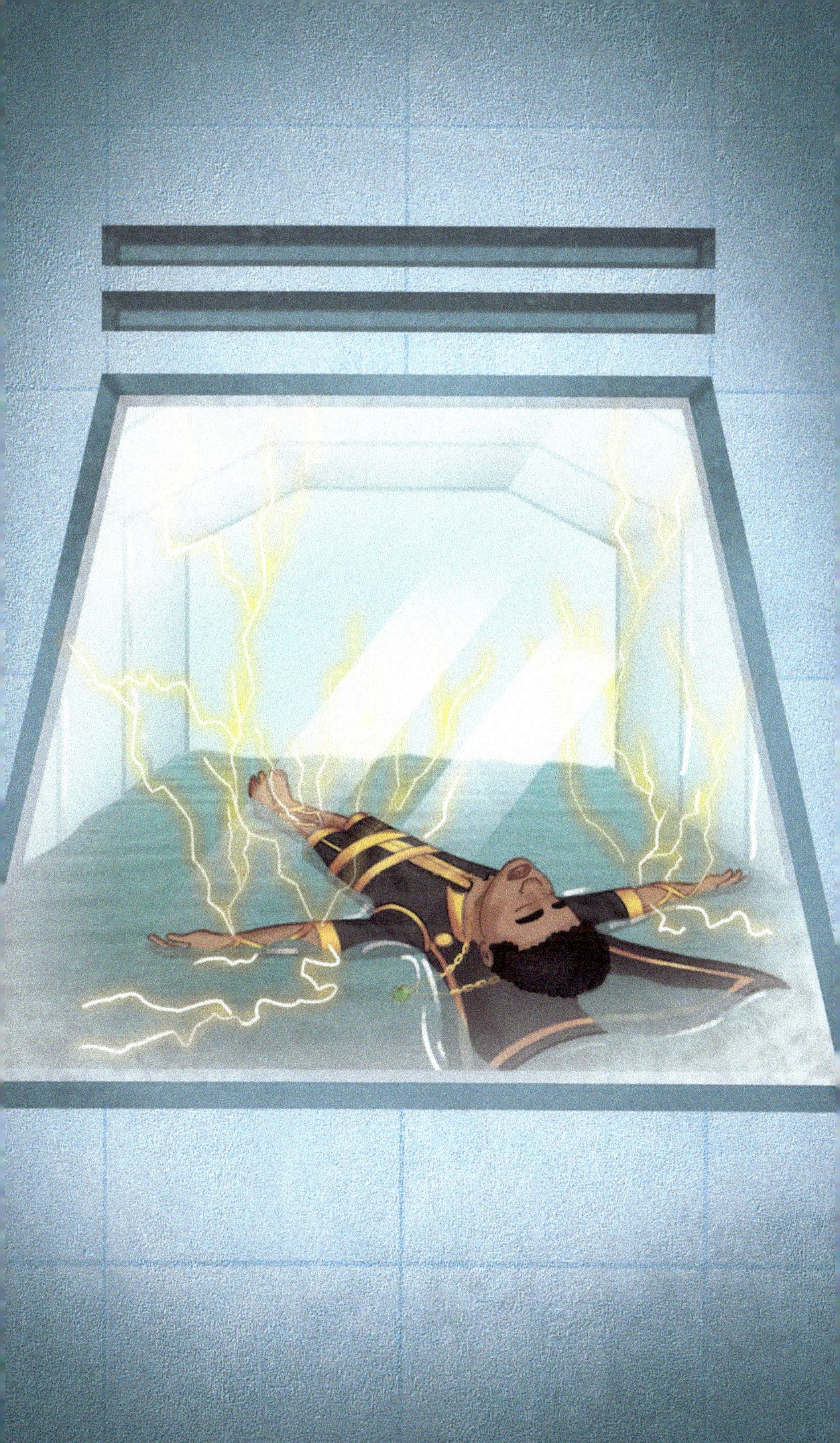

Suddenly on the release of his seventh breath. His body began to glow and you could even see electrical currents flowing through his veins. He stood up with amazement as he could feel the Zyo Armors activation underneath his skin.

The ancient ones then said to Tallrog, "we truly commended you on your bravery." They then gave him their blessings and farewell as Tallrog set forth on his way.

Chapter Two

HEART OF COURAGE

Now with the Zyo Armor activated inside Tallrog. He was able to ascend into space and head towards Planet Serutu. The first thing he noticed as he got closer to the planet was how beautiful and colorful it was. It was like no other planet in the galaxy from appearance.

Upon circling the planet he soon realized that it was indeed heavily guarded by soldiers everywhere. Though he has the Zyo Armor capable of fighting the soldiers, he feels it would be a long battle seeing that he is out numbered. Tallrog also came to the conclusion that he never wanted to hurt anybody also, so what should he do was the real question.

Tallrog decided he would do something that most people would deem insane but he felt in his heart it was the right thing to do. Which was head to one of the main entry's into the planet and talk to the soldiers of Serutu peacefully. He approached an army of soldiers upon entry and said "please do not be alarmed. I come peacefully."

The soldiers with their unique intimidating colorful armor stood there silently. Then a loud

voice was heard from behind them, "COME NO CLOSER INTRUDER!!!" The soldiers standing in a row turned to the side as a General by the name of Ucus approached Tallrog.

Tallrog sees the General approaching and says, "I am no intruder. My name is Tallrog and I've traveled from my planet Ta'Tubulas. I am on a quest to reach Planet Earth and I was told that your planet may have a special armor suit that could help me."

General Ucus replied, "You are speaking with General Ucus, protector of Serutu. Now why should me & my men help you." Tallrog then said, "because if i make it to planet Earth i will include you and your planet into the greatest story ever told for helping me.

I also have vowed to myself to create as much good in the universe as I possibly can by becoming the change for all of my people to see." Said Tallrog.

"Greatest story ever told huh," said General Ucus. "That's because no one ever makes it to planet Earth. What makes you think that you've got a chance?" Replied General Ucus.

Tallrog then said, "because I can feel it within me. I am destined for something much greater than just being absorbed by my planet possibly so soon. The Ancient ones from my planet said that on Earth I could possibly live forever."

General Ucus looked as if he was in deep thought. He then said, "did the Ancient ones also tell you that no one has ever put on the suit and survived. The Suit has proven to be much too powerful for anyone to handle.

The moment anyone has attempted to activate it, they perish into smoke and are never to be seen again. That is why we guard it so sacredly," said Ucus. "You actually think you've really got a chance?" Said Ucus.

Tallrog then looked at General Ucus and said

"I am peace, I am love, I have Gold inside my

blood. I am healthy, I am strong, I am worthy

to belong. I am destined, I am brave, I believe

I will see more days."

General Ucus looked at Tallrog and said,

"most people hear of what we hold on this

planet and they come attacking our planet

Serutu. They try to take what belongs to us.

You on the other hand came here respectfully

and instead spoke to me about your purpose in hope of a helping hand on your quest.

Risking your life. You also spoke of honoring our Beautiful Planet in return for our help. All this plus your desire to do much good in the universe makes me feel like you just might be worthy of surviving the suit.

You see we also never wanted the armor to fall into the wrong hands but you I really do like Tallrog." Said Ucus.

"For this I will lead you to the city of Ampullar where the Blasto Armor suit awaits you. We shall see if you really are who you say you are." Tallrog nodded his head to General Ucus and proudly said, "Thank You."

Chapter Three

THE POWER OF PEACE

General Ucus and some of his soldiers led Tallrog to this beautiful temple in the city of Ampullar. Upon approaching the temple Tallrog stood in amazement from how astounding the architecture was. It was like nothing he had ever seen before with all kinds of unique symbols embossed upon it.

The builders of Serutu sure do have some of the most creative brilliant minds, he thought to himself. "Right this way Tallrog," said General Ucus. Tallrog stepped into the temple and noticed a stairway that led up to the highest point of the temple.

Up there is a door that only general Ucus has the key to unlock. Behind it holds the most powerful suit in the universe. The Blasto Armor!

Before Tallrog could proceed up the stairway, one of Ucus soldiers by the name of Bolic yells, "YOU CAN'T BE THE CHOSEN ONE!" Ucus then yelled, "BOLIC STAND DOWN YOU HAVE MY ORDERS!"

Bolic then says, "but general how can we know for sure that he won't dishonor our planet. Or even use the suit as a weapon against us?" Ucus then said, "because I believe his heart is pure and worthy of an opportunity."

Bolic replies, "I'm sorry General but I can not take that chance, for I pledged my life to protect this planet and what belongs to us."

Bolic then rushes towards Tallrog with his powerful sword. He is immediately blown back upon impact by hitting this repulsive electric shield activated around Tallrog, that is surrounding his whole body.

Bolic's body now laid there almost lifeless on the ground with his eyes closed.

"I can't move," gasped Bolic. Tallrog then says unto General Ucus, "This was not what i wanted to do, but i had to protect myself."

General Ucus then said, "Bolic is one of my greatest men but I gave him instructions and he disobeyed. This is not your fault, Tallrog."

Tallrog still looked distraught. Tallrog then walked over to Bolic's body and placed one hand over his head. He said unto him, "through the life principle, which created all things. Through the very power that flows within my body and this universe. I command this man to be healed."

Suddenly Bolic's eyes opened. He began to move his limbs and attempted to stand. Tallrog extended his hand and helped him up. "I can't believe I'm healed. I attacked you...and yet you still spared my life, Tallrog.

Forgive me for I was obviously wrong about you." Said Bolic. Tallrog put one hand on Bolic's shoulder and said, "It's ok Bolic, for my purpose is to enhance and strengthen all life forms within the universe. It would never be to destroy them." Said Tallrog." "Thank you Tallrog," said Bolic. The Two shook

hands and then General Ucus said, "Well now

that this is all settled let us proceed up the

stairway." And so they did.

Chapter Four

SACRED NUMBER 9

They proceeded up the stairs and have now reached this wide door at the top of the temple. General Ucus places this unique star shaped key in the center of the door where the key shape was present. The key turned clockwise really fast and the door lifted up slowly.

There was a fluorescent glow coming from the whole room once the door was up. Tallrog looked ahead and immediately knew that his eyes were set on what had to be the Blasto Armor suit staring right back at him in the center of the room surrounded by Gold.

He stood there in amazement for a few seconds and then started to calm and courageously walk towards it. The body armor had a majestic teal and vibrant gold color. There was the number 9 on the left

chest plate and on

both shoulders of the armor. Tallrog looked at

Ucus and said, "what are these numbers for?

What does it mean?" General Ucus then said.

"The number 9 is a sacred number to our

planet.

It is a representation of cycle endings and new beginnings, essentially a symbol for transformation. I believe it also represents you Tallrog. The desire for transformation, and a new start is now within your reach."

Tallrog then said, "all i needed was an opportunity, a chance to become what I already knew myself to be internally.

I will honor this number deeply," said Tallrog. Tallrog smiled at General Ucus and then said, "I appreciate everything you've done to help me and now I must do what I came here to do."

The suit opened up from the back as Tallrog walked around it and stepped inside of it. The soldiers watched with shocking eyes. Immediately upon entry of the suit a blast of light blew the rooms walls down! The outside sky could now be seen around the top of the temple where they were. General Ucus and his soldiers picked themselves up from the rubble.

Dust particles began to fade from where Tallrog was standing and they could see that he still was inside of the suit. Only now his appearance was 6 times bigger than he currently was! General Ucus and his soldiers watched in disbelief.

"He survived! he survived!" Screamed Bolic, as they all started cheering and rushing towards Tallrog. "HOW DO YOU FEEL, TALLROG?" yelled Ucus. "I feel amazing, I feel immense power flowing through every part of my body!" Said Tallrog.

"Well you certainly look like it, you are incredibly HUGE Tallrog!" Yelled Bolic. Tallrog laughed and then said, "I am not sure what all I can do in this suit yet, but since you all have helped me. I will honor your planet's sacred number like I said I would. I will spend the next 9 months learning how to adjust to this suit and be of service. I will share every bit of this experience with you all here in Serutu!"

"Yeaaaaa!!!" They all yelled. "What an honorable man you are, Tallrog, a pure soul indeed," said General Ucus.

Chapter Five

MASTER OF THE UNIVERSE

The very next day Tallrog began to show more drastic changes. He could hear sounds from hundreds of miles away. He could see landscapes and people very clear from miles and miles away as well..

Did I forget to mention that he was also now

an even bigger giant than he was the day

prior. Having enormous height and strength

Tallrog built gigantic fortresses all over

Serutu for the soldiers to protect the planet.

He also built enormous temples for the people

of Serutu.

At these locations he believed it would be a

sacred place where the people of Serutu could

commune. They would practice mediation

and learn how to become healthier beings

through certain superfoods that he provided information upon.

They would also participate in group physical exercises there. Tallrog's planet Ta'Tubulas was big on these things which was a big reason why they were known to be some of the biggest and strongest beings already in the universe.

The people of Serutu loved Tallrog deeply for all that he had done for them. Approaching the 9th month Tallrog was almost bigger than the planet Serutu itself and he knew it was time for his departure. For he could now see and hear things from even planets away now. Upon one evening he leaned down from the clouds on this last day to speak to General Ucus. "It has been a privilege to have made such good friends with the people here in Serutu.

I will never forget what you did for me upon

my arrival," said Tallrog. "And we will never

forget what you did for us, Tallrog. It's not

just about the fortresses that you've created or

the temple's for my people. It is the beacon of

light and righteousness that you represent and

have

spread over the entire land. The way you believed in yourself is how I know that you are truly MOTU," said Ucus. "What is a MOTU?" Tallrog asked. "It means a MASTER OF THE UNIVERSE.

It is the name for the ones who we believe have managed much power and channeled it into a righteous purpose." Said Ucus. "I understand now, so in that case I believe we all have the opportunity to become MOTU from how I see it. For we all have the great power and ability to master ourselves, which is the universe." Said Tallrog. "Truly a wise soul you are Tallrog." Said Ucus. Tallrog then said, "from here on out I will take on a new title, seeing that I am in the 9th month of my time here.

Representing the transformation and evolution towards the next phase of my quest. I would like to remember and honor my planet for its sTRENghT, and honor your words of wisdom by changing my name to TRENT MOTU."

Said Tallrog. "I believe that to be a perfect fit for you, for i know now that you were the one spoken about, that would come here to Serutu as the light in our ancient tablets! It surely will be the greatest story ever told!" Screamed Ucus.

 "That you will forever have my word upon. Until the next time we meet again my good friend," said Tallrog. "Until the next time we meet again." replied General Ucus with a big smile.

Chapter Six

THE BREATH OF GRATITUDE

From that point is where TRENT MOTU was born. He then lifted his head back up to space, and started to ascend towards the planet Earth. The closer he got to planet Earth the smaller he started to become for some reason. By the time he had reached Earth's atmosphere his suit was slowly disappearing until it was all the way gone. At this time he had now shrunk down to being about 5"11" which is about the average height of a male on this planet.

 He landed in the Caribbean sea. Washing upon the shore seeming to be unconscious.

He then suddenly started to move and cough up water as he began to stand to his feet.

He gazed at the beautiful sun shining down on him and the tropical trees.

Thinking to himself about the bravery, the firm action and the strong will power it took for him to get here. He took in a deep breath, while embracing the feeling of being so blessed.

He began thinking to himself about how wonderful and empowering his whole journey had been. It is from here where the world will soon come to know and learn of the greatest story that will ever be told. TRENT MOTU, Master Of The Universe!!!

Acknowledgements

To the UNIVERSE, to my wonderful wife ROBIN, & to my incredible son TRENT. Thank you for being the greatest inspirations to my life and all of my life's work.

I want to also thank the rest of my family and all of the readers for your love & support.

Somebody once told me that I'm my son's hero.....that's likely true but my son is also mine. The reason is because when I see my son, he's a constant reminder of how I'm always supposed to be living my life. My son believes that he can do all things, he lives only for every present moment and he has no fear of anything in the universe. Thank you my son for inspiring me & the rest of the world!

Afterword

The truth is....we are all masters of the universe. The reason being is that we all have the ability to create our own realities. If you believe this for yourself to be true, then help one another discover the MOTU that's

hidden deep within us already. I

hope the lessons from this book can

serve as a great guide towards your

own personal journeys and lives

together!

www.ingramcontent.com/pod-product-compliance
Lightning Source LLC
Chambersburg PA
CBHW040840010826
48978CB00012BB/843